Dear Elsie
It's been lovely to have you in
Reception this year.
Good luck in Year One!
Lots of love

Miss McVey
♡.
Mrs Openshaw
xx

IMAGINE THAT™

Licensed exclusively to Imagine That Publishing Ltd
Tide Mill Way, Woodbridge, Suffolk, IP12 1AP, UK
www.imaginethat.com
Copyright © 2019 Imagine That Group Ltd
All rights reserved
0 2 4 6 8 9 7 5 3 1
Manufactured in China

Retold by Sarah Lucy
Illustrated by Kimberley Barnes

ISBN 978-1-78958-197-3

A catalogue record for this book is available from the British Library

Snow White

The Brothers Grimm

Retold by Sarah Lucy
Illustrated by Kimberley Barnes

Once upon a time, on a cold winter's day, a beautiful queen sat at her window, sewing.

As the queen watched the snow fall, she began to dream about the daughter she had always wished for.

'If I had a daughter, her skin would be as white as the falling snow and her hair as black as a raven,' the queen said, longingly.

'I would call her Snow White.'

The queen's wish soon came true and she had a little girl. The Queen named her Snow White.

The happiness was not to last long, as the queen sadly died.

Before long, the king married again. The new queen was beautiful but vain, and not a good mother to Snow White.

Every day, she asked her magic mirror, 'Mirror, mirror, on the wall, who is the fairest of us all?'

The mirror would always reply, 'Oh queen, you are the fairest in all the land.'

As the years passed, Snow White grew more and more beautiful. One day, the queen asked the mirror, 'Mirror, mirror, on the wall, who is the fairest of us all?'

To her horror, the mirror replied, 'Oh queen, you are a beauty, it's true, but Snow White has grown much fairer than you.'

'This can't be true!' cried the queen, and she ordered her guard to take Snow White far away from the castle at once.

The guard led Snow White far away from the castle into the deep, dark forest and left her there. Snow White was lost and very afraid.

Soon she came to a small cottage. Cautiously, she opened the door and crept inside.

Inside the cottage, Snow White saw a table surrounded by seven small chairs and set with seven plates.

Upstairs, she found seven small beds. Snow White was so tired that she couldn't resist lying down and she soon fell fast asleep.

Later that evening, the owners of the cottage returned. When Snow White woke, she was surprised to see seven friendly dwarfs staring back at her!

'You mustn't be afraid of us,' said the first dwarf. 'We will look after you.'

Snow White was happy in her new home and she enjoyed helping the seven dwarfs with their chores.

Back at the castle, the Queen was delighted that Snow White had gone. She spoke to the magic mirror again.

To her horror, the mirror replied, 'Oh queen, you are a beauty, it's true, but Snow White is far, far fairer than you.'

Furiously, the Queen set out
to find Snow White.

After searching for a long time,
the queen arrived in disguise
at the dwarfs' cottage.

Snow White trusted the old lady
and let her in for a drink.

'Thank you, my dear,' said the queen brightly. 'Let me give you this lovely comb to show my thanks.'

But Snow White didn't realise that the comb was poisoned! As she brushed her hair, she fell to the floor.

When the dwarfs arrived home they found Snow White. To their relief, her eyes opened and she told them all about the old lady and the comb.

'It was the wicked queen!' said the dwarfs. 'You must promise us that you will never open the door to a stranger again!'

Back at the castle, the queen asked the mirror again, 'Mirror, mirror, on the wall, who is the fairest of us all?'

To her horror, the mirror replied, 'Oh queen, you are a beauty, it's true, but Snow White is far, far fairer than you.'

Angrier than ever, the queen charged back to the cottage in the forest, this time disguised as an old man selling shiny red apples.

'Open the door, dear,' said the queen in a gruff voice.

'I don't let strangers in,' replied Snow White.

'I'll just leave an apple on the windowsill for you to enjoy later,' said the queen, and she left.

Snow White couldn't resist taking a bite of the delicious apple, but it was poisoned, and she fell to the floor!

When the seven dwarfs returned home, they found Snow White, but this time, she did not wake up.

'Our beautiful Snow White has been sent to sleep by the evil queen,' they cried.

The dwarfs laid Snow White on a bed of beautiful flowers and sat beside her every day, waiting for her to wake up.

After many years, a handsome prince came across the dwarfs' cottage. As he gazed at Snow White, he instantly fell in love.

Suddenly, Snow White's eyes opened!

When the evil queen realised that Snow White was alive, she ran into the forest, never to be seen again.

As for Snow White and her handsome prince – they lived happily ever after.